Peter's Power

Written by **Shirley Johnston**

Illustrated by **Chad Thompson**

Enjoy !

Shirley Johnston

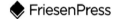 FriesenPress

One Printers Way
Altona, MB R0G 0B0
Canada

www.friesenpress.com

ISBN
978-1-03-916804-6 (Hardcover)
978-1-03-916803-9 (Paperback)
978-1-03-916805-3 (eBook)

1. Juvenile Fiction, Social Issues, Homelessness & Poverty

Distributed to the trade by The Ingram Book Company

Dylan so enjoyed listening to my stories about life
experiences and how to help others.

He loved this story and begged me to one day
make it into a storybook he could keep forever.

I promised him I would, and therefore I
developed this book.

I hope you enjoy this story
as much as Dylan did.

Regards,
Shirley Johnston.

Once upon a time,

there was a little boy called Peter.

His dad made **shoes** and his mother made **bread**.

Peter's father was a very good shoemaker and would make all kinds of different shoes. His mother was very good at bread-making and would make different types of bread.

Peter's family did not have much money, but they worked hard and made enough money to buy what they needed.

One day, Peter and his family moved. Peter had to go to a new school. He was very nervous, but his mom and dad told him, "Work hard, do your best, and listen to your teacher, if you do that, everything will be okay".

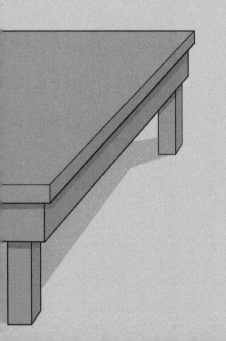

The day came for Peter to start at his new school. He made lots of friends and he liked his teacher. Everything had gone well—except lunchtime. He went home and told his parents all about it.

Everyone in his class sat in a circle
together to eat their lunches.
All the other children had

so much

to eat in their lunch boxes,
but Peter only had two slices of bread.
The new friends he had made teased him
because he didn't have anything else to eat.

Peter's father said, "Peter, you tell your
friends that you are very lucky because
your mother makes your bread for you
with lots of love, you are a lucky boy to
have a mom that can do that for you".

Peter went to school the next day feeling
better than when he had left the previous day,
At lunchtime, when he and his classmates were
all in the circle having lunch, he decided
to tell his friends how special his bread was.

"You know". "Peter said, "my mom makes
my bread for me with lots of love,
I'm happy she can do this for me,
and my dad makes my shoes".

His friends stopped teasing him after that.

A few weeks passed and another new boy started at Peter's school. He was very shy at lunchtime. He sat in the circle with all the other children, but he didn't have a lunch box. He just sat and watched all the other children eat.

When Peter saw this, he got up from the other side of the circle, walked over to the little boy, sat beside him, and spoke. "Hi, my name is Peter. Would you like to share my bread with me? My mom always makes my bread and it tastes really good!".

"Yes, please," said the other little boy". "My name is Mark, and I am so hungry. My mom and dad have no work because there aren't any jobs available, so we just don't have enough money for lots of food".

Peter gave Mark one of his slices of bread. Mark enjoyed the bread so much, he said,

"wow, this is the best bread I have ever had".

"That's great". Peter said, "I will bring more tomorrow so we can have lunch together again". Mark was very happy.

When Peter got home, he said to his mom, "Please, Mom, can you give me more bread to take to school? I made a new friend named Mark. His parents have no work and no money, so he has no food to eat during lunchtime".

His mom said, "of course, I will give you more slices of bread—two slices for you and two for Mark. I am very proud of you for sharing your lunch, Peter".

The next day, Peter went to school with two lunch boxes, One for Mark and one for himself, He was very happy they both had two slices of bread to eat at lunchtime.

Mark said to Peter, "**this is the best bread I've ever had! Your mom is a very good baker**".

Then Peter said, "my mom wants to know if she can make bread for your family, so you all have something to eat".

"That would be so great!" Mark said.

That weekend, Peter's mom made two loaves of bread for Mark's family. She then asked the boy's teacher for Mark's address so she could drop off the loaves of bread at their house.

Instead of giving Peter's mom the address, the teacher offered to take the loaves of bread herself. She would collect the loaves of bread from Peter's house and take them to Mark's house.

The teacher was delighted to be helping. She was even more delighted when she arrived at Peter's house and saw the beautiful shoes Peter's dad had made.

The teacher loved one pair of shoes so much, she asked if she could buy them. Peter's dad said, "of course". The teacher was so happy to have such a beautiful pair of shoes.

She thanked Peter's parents
for the bread they made
for Mark's family, and her
wonderful new shoes.
She then delivered the loaves
of bread to Mark's house;

His family was
very grateful.

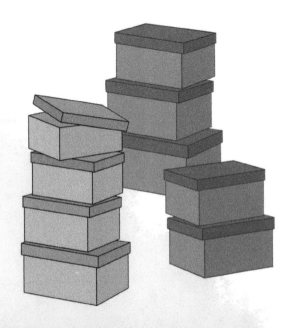

On Monday morning, the teacher wore her **beautiful new shoes** to school.

Everyone just loved her shoes and asked her where she got them.

She was so happy to tell them that she bought them from Peter's father, who made many beautiful pairs of shoes.

After that day, Peter's father had so many calls for pairs of shoes,

he could barely keep up!

At the same time, Peter's mom had many orders for her tasty bread.

Peter's father realized he needed help, so he asked Mark's dad if he would like to work with him.

Peter's family became good friends with Mark's family and Peter's mother gave them more bread.

Mark's dad was so happy!

He said he would love to do that.

Then Peter's mom realized she needed help as well, so Mark's mom began helping her to make bread.

They were all so happy, and as time went by, the two families opened a big **shoe factory** and a **bakery**. Both businesses did very well, making everyone lots of money so they could buy everything they needed.

This was a great lesson for Peter and Mark, who learned the value of working hard and helping others.

The End

CPSIA information can be obtained
at www.ICGtesting.com
Printed in the USA
LVHW011908090623
749086LV00002B/5